Big Shark's Halloween Mystery

To Robbie and Krebs
—S.M.

ISBN-13: 978-0-545-00237-0
ISBN-10: 0-545-00237-0

12 11 10 9 8 7 6 5 4 3 2 1   7 8 9 10 11 12/0

Printed in the U.S.A.
First printing, October 2007

Book design by Jennifer Rinaldi Windau

Big Shark's Halloween Mystery

by Steve Metzger

Illustrated by Cedric Hohnstadt

SCHOLASTIC INC.

New York   Toronto   London   Auckland   Sydney
Mexico City   New Delhi   Hong Kong   Buenos Aires

Chomp, the lemon shark, couldn't wait to go trick-or-treating.

"Mommy! Mommy!" he called out. "I want to put on my

Halloween costume."

Chomp's mother swam over and helped him with his pirate hat and eye patch.

"Now, I'm the world famous Pirate of the Sea!" Chomp said as he admired himself in the mirror. "Can we trick-or-treat now, Mommy? Can we, please?"

"Okay," Chomp's mother said with a smile. "Let's go. And remember," she added, "don't frighten the little fish."

"I don't want to. But how can I show them I'm not scary?" Chomp asked.

Chomp's mother thought for a moment. "Just wave and smile," she said. "That way they'll know you're a friendly pirate shark."

"All right, Mommy," Chomp replied as he grabbed his

Halloween bag and raced off to get some candy. Chomp swam

past a coral reef.

Chomp looked ahead. A group of angel fish were swimming
straight toward him. *Wave and smile*, Chomp remembered. The
school of angelfish saw Chomp's friendly face and smiled back.

A few seconds later, he arrived at a neighbor's home.

"Trick-or-treat!" Chomp called out.

Mandy, the moray eel, swam out of her cave with a piece of seashell candy and dropped it in his bag. "Happy Halloween, Chomp!" she said. "Have fun!"

"Thank you," Chomp called out. Next, he swam toward a
sunken ship while his mother waited patiently behind. All
at once, he saw hundreds of yellow tang and butterfly fish
swimming right toward him. He began to wave and smile,
but they were too frightened to wave back.

"What's the matter?" Chomp shouted. "Why are you so scared?"
But they were already gone. *I wonder why they are so
frightened,* Chomp thought. *I've got to find out what scared
them. It's a real mystery!*

Chomp glided over to a couple of loggerhead sea turtles. "Do you know what scared all those little fish?" he asked. But the sea turtles were too busy playing tricks on each other to answer.

He swam over to a polka-dot grouper, waving and smiling. The grouper smiled back, but then his eyes opened wide and he quickly darted off.

"Come back!" Chomp called out. "Why are you swimming away?"

Chomp heard a noise and turned around. All at once, he was face-to-face with a fang tooth, the scariest fish he had ever seen.

"Are...are...are you wearing a Halloween mask?" Chomp whispered.

The fang tooth shook his head.

"Well, I...I...I'll be seeing you," Chomp stuttered as he began to swim away.

"Don't go!" the fang tooth said. "I won't hurt you. My name is Fangy. What's yours?"

Gathering his courage, Chomp inched back. "My name is Chomp. I don't think I've ever seen you before."

"That's right," Fangy answered. "I live in the deepest part of the ocean, where there's no sunlight at all. Since today is Halloween, I wanted to go trick-or-treating. But it looks like I'm scaring everyone. I guess I'll go back home."

"No, don't," Chomp said. "We can go trick-or-treating together."

"Really?" Fangy *exclaimed.* "That's great!"

"But first I want you to meet my mommy."

As they swam to where his mother was waiting, Chomp taught Fangy how to smile and wave at the little fish so he wouldn't scare them.

But when they arrived, Chomp's mother jumped up in fright.

"Don't be scared, Mommy," Chomp explained. "Fangy is my new friend. He wants to celebrate Halloween. He's the reason why all those little fish were so scared. Fangy didn't know he was supposed to smile and wave."

"I see," Chomp's mother replied with a smile. "If you're going to trick-or-treat, Fangy will need a costume. What should he be for Halloween?"

Chomp looked around and found a cone-shaped seashell.

"I know!" Chomp said. "He can be a silly clown. Fangy, do you like that idea?"

Fangy nodded.

Chomp's mother placed the seashell on Fangy's head, gave him a red nose, and they were off. Chomp reminded Fangy about smiling and waving when they passed the little fish.

It was Chomp's best Halloween ever! He got lots of yummy treats . . . and he made a new friend, too!